NO HENS ALLOWED

To Ian, with love — D.S.

For Ethan, Miles, Owen and Tiggy — K.L.

OXFORD
UNIVERSITY PRESS

Great Clarendon Street, Oxford OX2 6DP

Oxford University Press is a department of the University of Oxford.
It furthers the University's objective of excellence in research, scholarship,
and education by publishing worldwide in

Oxford New York

Auckland Cape Town Dar es Salaam Hong Kong Karachi
Kuala Lumpur Madrid Melbourne Mexico City Nairobi
New Delhi Shanghai Taipei Toronto

With offices in
Argentina Austria Brazil Chile Czech Republic France Greece
Guatemala Hungary Italy Japan Poland Portugal Singapore
South Korea Switzerland Thailand Turkey Ukraine Vietnam

Text copyright © 2013 Debbie Singleton
Illustrations copyright © 2013 Kristyna Litten
The moral rights of the author and artist have been asserted

Database right Oxford University Press (maker)

First published 2013
First published in paperback 2014

British Library Cataloguing in Publication Data available

ISBN: 978-0-19273415-0 (paperback)

10 9 8 7 6 5 4 3 2 1

Printed in China

Paper used in the production of this
book is a natural, recyclable product made
from wood grown in sustainable forests.
The manufacturing process conforms
to the environmental regulations
of the country of origin

BUDD'S
FARM

FREE RANGE
EGGS
FOR SALE

PIGEON PIE, OH MY!

DEBBIE SINGLETON · KRISTYNA LITTEN

OXFORD
UNIVERSITY PRESS

On market day Farmer Budd jumped out of bed as soon as the cock crowed. He milked the cows. He collected eggs.

He picked a bowlful of cherries so that Mrs Budd could bake cherry pies.

BUDD 1

Then he started to spread his nets to protect the rest of his cherries.

'Rotten rodents!' he muttered. 'Those rats have nibbled holes in my nets.'
But he didn't have time to mend them . . .

. . . he had other jobs to do before he could set off for market.
He remembered to feed the animals.

the bull

the donkey

the sheepdog

the tiny chick

He remembered
to load up the trailer
with milk and eggs.

Oops!

He remembered
to give the old scarecrow
a new straw hat.

Munch!
The old tweed
trousers disappeared.

Chomp!
Down went the saggy
baggy red jumper.

Crunch!
That was the end
of the new straw hat.

All that was left were two sticks
in the middle of the cornfield . . .

which made a perfect
perch for five peckish
pigeons who happened
to be passing.

'That greedy goat,' said the donkey. 'Look what he's done! We can't let those pigeons eat all the corn!'

'I can't toss them out,' said the bull sadly. 'I would trample the corn.'

'I can't round them up,' said the sheepdog. 'Chasing birds makes me dizzy.'

But the
tiny chick whispered,
'I have a plan.'
Then she raised her voice just loud
enough for the pigeons to hear.

'I see the farmer has made a lovely perch
in the cornfield to attract the birds.
It must be pigeon pie day today.'

She winked a tiny wink
and the donkey grinned.
'Pigeon pie!' he said. 'Oh my!'

The pigeons turned to listen.

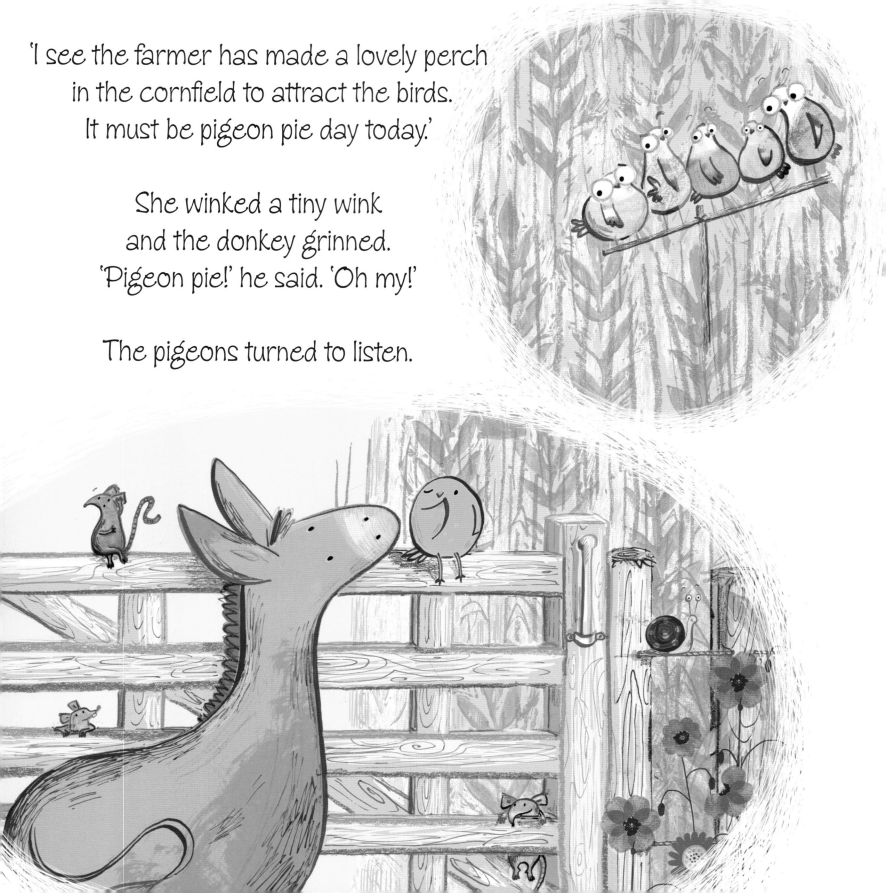

'I see the farmer has got out his bird-catching nets.
It must be pigeon pie day today,' said the chick.

The sheepdog's eyes gleamed.
'Pigeon pie! Oh my!'

The pigeons looked
at the nets and gulped.

Then the tiny chick
turned to the bull.
'I see the farmer's wife is
making pastry. It must be
pigeon pie day today.'

The bull snorted excitedly.
'Pigeon pie! Oh my!'

The

pigeons

stared,

wide-eyed,

towards

the kitchen

window . . .

and shot into the air . . .

like feathered cannonballs.

'We did it!' cheered the animals, just as Farmer Budd returned.

And they told him all about the greedy goat and the petrified pigeons.

'My clever corn-savers,' said the farmer,
patting the bull, the sheepdog, the donkey, and the tiny chick.

'I think you all deserve
a piece of fresh cherry pie.'

'Cherry pie!' chorused the animals.
'Oh my!'

'But none for you!' Farmer Budd glared at the goat.

Mrs Budd made the best cherry pies. She remembered everything her mother had taught her.

How to mix the lightest pastry.

How to roll it smooth and flat.

How to fill the pie just right.

And bake it to a perfect golden brown.

But she forgot one thing . . .
the window.

No, two things . . .
the window . . .
and the goat.

'Oh no you don't!'
said the tiny chick.
'Not this time!'

BUDD'S
FARM

FREE RANGE
EGGS
SOLD OUT

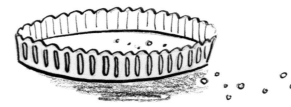